# `for the broken soul

## Breaking. Healing. Loving

## FÁTIMA FRANCESA

ISBN: 9781799027256

# Dedication

to the men that couldn't appreciate me
to the ones that did me wrong;
i'm sorry you misunderstood me
i'm sorry you overlooked the magic in me.

thank you for inspiring the words in this book.
i'm sorry you failed to realize i was more than a look.
you realized what you lost, but i'm afraid it's far too late.

i'll leave these words printed for you to soak in,
let it marinate.

to the love of my life,
thank you for loving me so purely,
all of me.
thank you for loving my chaotic mind.
this is the sweet beautiful love i dreamed of,
unrefined.

to all my broken girls,
keep healing.
keep loving.

# Table of Contents

# Preface

i wrote this book and i told myself ..
turn your pain into a purpose
turn your struggles into success
turn your anger into art
turn your crying into a creation
turn the madness into a masterpiece

.. i turned my lessons into a work of literature

# Elements:

she was an element.

she was the type whose presence could be felt without ever having to press skin against you.

she was like water.
soft enough to nurture you
deep enough to reach the furthest corners of your soul
and powerful enough to withstand any storm.

she was fire.
enough to keep you warm
hot enough to send flames through your body
bright enough to light the world
strong enough to burn you down if she needed.

she was wind.
gentle enough to soothe you
loud enough to cause a storm
and strong enough to break you down.

her brain carried books
her mind carried stories few would understand.

she was a whole mixture of your elements.

*... and still you lost her*

# The Breaking

go to sleep.
let your heart rest tonight.
you've been thinking too long and hard. & he is just not worth it
anymore.

at one point, you get tired of trying for those that don't try for you. you become resistant. & eventually, you have to learn to  let it go in peace.

the way he walked in and out of your life.
leaving scars on your heart. he said it was love. that's not love girl, it's
destruction.

the next time he comes back, let him go for good. you don't deserve
the confusion, you don't deserve his altered definition of love.

your heart is not a revolving door. it's not meant to be walked on or
abused. it's meant to be cherished and treated so delicately.

i used to crave closure from you just so i could be sure it would end
once and for all.

but you kept coming back. each time cutting a little deeper. don't
you know how much destruction you caused?

i wish you would just leave for good
i'm tired of you coming back to ruin my mood

every time you come back and say that you love me
you miss me
you need me
but you left, remember.

keep that same energy, and please just stop draining me.

don't fall for someone incapable of loving you the way you deserve to
be loved.
half love, is not love.
inconsistency, is not love.
to love someone fully and not have it reciprocate, is not love. it's
confusion. it's destruction.

- *blurred lines*

too young.
too early.
your last love left you broken.
you don't trust love.
i get it.
you can't set yourself up to be hurt again.
i get it.

*- young love*

you were never too much.
you were never not enough.

you were misunderstood.
he didn't take the time to search deeper.
he didn't even get to explore everything you had to offer.
he simply wasn't ready for all the magic that you came with.
he left you empty.

*- it wasn't you*

i hope you realize that you're enough.
he will realize it too. but it'll be far too late.
because you'll be with someone who realized it from the start.

- *no second chances*

he lost you.
you lost nothing.

you should be proud of yourself.
breaking, and picking yourself back up.
that courage looks so good on you.
your softness is not a weakness.
your kindness is your strength.

how brave of you to heal yourself
how brave of you to allow love once again
you've been through so much, and still you stand.
i hope you realize how courageous that makes you

- *resilience*

i know it hurts.
when you think you found your forever
and it ends up just being a moment.
a feeling, temporary comfort
a fling.


you invested all your time
you put your heart back on the line.
you opened up, and he let you down.
you thought he'd be the one.
you thought he'd prove to be different
but still, he let you down.

- *ended too soon*

i told you all my secrets.
i told you how my heart was scarred.
and you still walked all over my heart.
left it in pieces to revive itself.

no oxygen, now i can't breathe.
no heart activity, it was dead.
my wounds too deep to stitch back up

i must be addicted to the rush.
so i can revive it myself

i must love allowing my heart to crush
time and time again.

*- CPR*

you know what,
i'm starting to feel like love is a lot like handing someone a full loaded
gun aimed at your heart,

and trusting them not to pull the trigger.

- *what love means to me*

man, i loved you so hard. i gave you my all.
i wanted to ride with you till the end.
and still you walked away.

after dark.

when all the thoughts flow into your mind.

you think about all the damage that has been done.

how you will never fall in love again.

it feels like your heart is slowly dying, as you try to piece the shreds

that are left of it.

you feel like part of you is gone.

it physically hurts.

it's called heartbreak, girl.

just hold on and let it pass.

trust issues.
the lies, the inconsistency, the games.
you let your guard down.
you let him in and it broke you down.

here's the thing about your love.

strong, pure, real.

you have to understand that some men will never be ready to accept

something as real as you.

they get scared. maybe even intimidated.

they can't handle how you're so soft inside, and a little rough around

the edges.

it was never about you.

you are golden.

let it go.

how can i be everything to you one day, and the next i am nothing.
you leave with no word.
did i ever mean anything to you?
the inconsistent behavior, that is what kills me the most.
the silence, it cuts so deep.

all you did was cut deeper into my soul with every thrust.
we were never making love.

my knees ached at the thought of holding down a man who only
wanted to hold me down for the night.

my spine sore. my shoulders tender, my neck ached at carrying all the
expectations.

my throat hurt from all the times i had to scream my worth.

i ate pineapple, bathed in luxury water, but nothing tasted better than
the loyalty.

my body felt like a map to you. and you had no idea how to navigate
it.

lost, blind.

*- one night stand*

can we just rest tonight.
quiet down our minds.
stop thinking about the what if's and why's.
stop worrying about nothing.
stop thinking about people who aren't thinking about us.
stop thinking about why it didn't work out or what you did wrong.

let's close all the open tabs in our minds.
press delete. esc. backspace. shut down.

the human heart. my favorite organ.
breaks and still beats. revives itself.
it even dies sometimes.
the oxygen gets cut off.
the blood doesn't reach all the vessels.
it stops for a moment.
and then it comes back.
stronger than before.
stitched back together.
wounds bandaged up.

- *resuscitation*

you stopped talking to me.
you just went silent.
no explanations.
the confusion, misunderstandings, and unspoken truths.
maybe that's what hurt me the most.

- *silent rejection*

your relationship is a mess. you don't have to hear it from me because
you know this is directed towards you. i know you feel worthless, but
you stick around because the pain is familiar.
somewhere out there, someone is waiting to find you, to give you
everything you think you don't deserve because you're used to the
mistreatment. i still see your crown. you just need to readjust it and
see it yourself.

- *someone's dream girl*

the wrong type of love can change you forever.
the right type of love can hold you together.

*- choose wisely*

why do you keep allowing yourself to be continuously played with?
can you pause and ask yourself this question for a moment?

- *you're not an instrument*

real love.
the type that can leave her soul wild. free her spirit. ignite her mind.
free her body. & calm her storms.

we were both broken, i felt that.
we both had turbulent pasts.

your broken was attracted to my broken.

your atoms were attracted to mine.

- *it was chemistry*

i feel like my heart nearly breaks all over again at the thought of talking to someone new.

knowing they will never be you.

telling me they're different but they never come through.

setting myself up for hurt feelings and disappointment like i always do.

- *maybe i never fully healed*

i fell asleep next to you.

dreamed about you.

woke up next to you with your arms around me.

- *bliss*

baby girl, just focus on your goals.

follow your dreams wildly and unapologetically.

these men are confused.

stop delaying your passions because of distractions.

*- just reminding you*

it's a little crazy, how i thought you were the one.
& once i finally left, it turned out that the whole time you were
holding me back, restricting me, depriving me even, from finding the
love that you were incapable of giving me.

- *broke loose from the chains*

it's not our fault we have a wall around our heart.

it's a natural process built from resentment, rejection,
disappointment, heartbreak, lies, pain, inconsistency.

but the women with the guards up love the hardest.

you might just need to dig a little deeper to get to her heart.

*- security system*

i can see all of your scars.
let me show you mine too.
i'd like to hear more about your past.
i'll tell you my stories too.
don't worry.
i won't be the one to re-open the wounds that you've healed.
i've stitched all of mine back together.
i'd like to help you too.

- *soul surgery*

i know it feels like you're the only one struggling for love.
with an aching heart.
wondering where everything went wrong.
even blaming yourself at times.

you're not alone. stay patient.

chances are your best kiss and strongest love haven't even happened
yet.

*- real love takes time*

i didn't believe in magic until i met you.
you reached through my chest and gave my heart life again.

- *world's greatest act*

your skin against mine, laughing until 1pm, eating fruits in bed,
falling in and out of sleep together

*- a sunday morning*

the girl you took for granted will heal on her own and eventually discover you were never actually a loss.

she was the type of imperfect that someone needed.

you said i was a different type of girl.

you said you wanted more of me.

but then you treated me like a moment. & then we evaporated into nothing.

i think we had the wifi on but the connection was weak.

*- failed signal*

a ghost watches all your moves, but doesn't speak to you in real life.

a ghost comes back the second they sense you are happy with someone else.

a ghost is someone that still wants a connection with you, but is too weak to communicate misunderstandings.

if you ever go ghost on me, you can stay in the afterlife.

*- i don't speak to the dead*

a man that you can share business ideas, creative ideas, visualizations, and openly talk about goals with.

that's a man you need to keep by your side.

- *king for a queen*

stop bending over backwards for a man who refuses to do anything for you, who puts in the bare minimum, no effort.

stop trying harder and harder when he's not even trying for you. stop treating him like a boyfriend or husband when he's comfortable treating you like a secret, a getaway, a moment.

- *move tf on*

don't interrupt the woman who is working to put the pieces of her
heart back together.

healing wounds.
bettering herself.
moving forward.
how could you just walk in to her life, claiming to be different, re-
opening the scars, feeding lies, and cutting her soul once again.

at this point, you're a different type of low.

let me put my walls back up.

let me shield and guard my heart once again.

i let you in a little too far.

i feel exposed.

my heart feels naked.

my soul feels like it's been stripped down

i think i let you in a little too far

and i don't like it anymore.

i know you may feel easily replaceable at times.

he moved on so fast.

he has someone new already

& he's acting like it'll last.

you're one of a kind remember.

you're a breath of fresh air
like that first snowflake in December

there is no else like you
you will never be replaceable

you're a whole diamond

i could've been everything for you if only you would have let me.

i mean, i remember the way you looked at me the first time you met me.

different, rare, a dream girl you said.

but you'd rather have me for one night instead.

let's be real.
you were never ready for real love
and that's where it all went wrong

i'm not the type of person to give up on someone so easily.

i will work with you, learn you, i'll even try and heal your past wounds and that's where i've always messed up.

i don't abandon people and just act like there was never a thing between us.

that's why it always hurts when someone gives up so easily on me.

like did i ever mean anything to you or it was just a fling?

i was attracted to your brokenness.
i wanted to be the missing piece to your puzzle.
i should've left when you said you were looking for your happiness.

instead i stayed, and made my own mind a mess.

see my heart is so big, i wanted to give you a chance,
i wanted to participate in your healing.
instead, i learned you can't get caught up in a feeling.

healthy relationships occur when two individuals are comfortable
with themselves.

yeah, we're all damaged.
but your heart should be somewhat stable before you attempt real
love.

a healthy relationship involves nurturing and watering each other's
souls.
you must continue to grow individually
and as a couple too, after all.

that type of love is magical.
stop settling for just CO-EXISTING with someone.

have you ever thought that the reason you're struggling to love yourself is because you're not your own "type?"

here you are trying to be like the other girls. look like them, talk like them, make the same moves as them.

here you are wasting time from self-love because you're blinded by what you think you "should be".

the love of your life is right in front of you.

it's you.

the type of love that comes when you aren't looking is on another level.

you're spending too much time looking, and not enough time living.

let it flow naturally.

do you. work hard. spoil yourself. date yourself and spend time with yourself.

timing is everything. it's gonna come when you least expect it and it'll be so worth it.

is it too much risk to fall into the same type of deep love
only to experience the same type of deep pain?

but see, that's a risk i'm willing to take for you.

for the only risk here is missing out on the way you light my whole
heart in a disneyland show of fireworks

- *risks*

i find it a little crazy how amidst the chaos in my mind, you bring me peace.

you discovered the deepest corners of my soul, which such precision and expertise.

it's something about you that calms me down,

i take slower breaths and exhale my worries.

all i know is i need you around, but no hurry.

- *what he does to me*

you emptied yourself and gave up your whole entire soul for someone
who didn't even shed a tear over you.

that's why it stings.
because sometimes we want them to feel what we feel.

we want them to hurt the way they made us hurt.

*mirrored emotions*

he only says i love you and i miss you when he wants some.

he always knows how to work his way back into your life doesn't he?

this is where you have to draw the line.

you may want him back too, but you certainly don't need him.

i stripped down my soul,
and to you i was just another girl.

am i hard to love?
it's just .. i kind of want you in my life forever
soo ..
don't leave when it gets hard.
don't leave on the days you feel like i'm hard to love.

can you love me on my worst days too?

can you promise you'll still be there and not walk away?

if someone is meant for you,
fate will find a way to bring that person back into your life.

it doesn't matter if they're oceans away,
continents away.

it doesn't matter if years have gone by,
life happened,
and you fell off.

it may even have been wrong timing.

maybe you both weren't ready at the time.
but if that person matches to your soul
and they are the one that the universe sent for you,
they will come right back into your life
and you will pick back up,
maybe even stronger than before.

- *timing*

i bent over backwards carrying the weight of my expectations from
you

and still you managed to disappoint me in every way possible.

i miss your smile.

i miss your voice.

my body misses yours.

my atoms are craving your atoms.

why did it have to end so soon.

i wasn't done loving on you yet

don't hurt anyone that you care for.

it only takes a few moments to create the damage

and it can take years to heal

you're too young too drown in sadness,
you don't even know how to swim yet.

heartbreak comes early a lot of times.
you learn about pain and broken trust.

you learn what it feels like to open up your soul
only to have someone break it down.

but i wish you would take these years to learn about yourself, grow in
your strength, and learn what it's like to be happy on your own.

you're just too young to waste those precious years.

you keep falling and getting bruised
you're taking the helmet off way too early.

you're barely learning how to ride the bike.

did you not see the way she looked into your eyes,
as if she was trying to scream out loud all the hurt she had been
through?

she looked at you so deep, like she was trying to find all the answers
in your eyes.

did you not feel the way she would hug you so tight?
as if she was trying to tell you not to be another one to let her go?

do you not remember how she would hold on to your hand?
trace all the bones and joints of your body, feeling the skin on the
surface,
nothing sexual, but almost as if she was ready to hold you down in
every way.

i guess you might see it and understand when it's too late.
you might have been blinded by sudden attention from someone else.

one day you'll see it though. you'll see it when you look for her in
every last one of your lovers. and they're just not her.

all these people walked in and out of my life leaving scars that were uninvited.

now they're gone and i have this weird feeling inside of me like if something has ignited.

as if i met my old self again and was reunited.

*i missed you*

those tough alpha women with the guards up will soften up  when you love them properly.

and then it's a whole different world you have tapped into.

just learn how to uncover that top layer first.

there are wounds she had to heal on her own.

that's why there's a shield around her heart.

*she's not cold*

she'll always be that rare opportunity that you could not appreciate.

she'll always be that one girl that you never forget.

time will go on, and you'll still find her on your mind.

don't ever forget, she was one of a kind.

your next girl may be all looks, but no soul.

you lost a real one, she was ready to make you feel whole.

i don't cry over little boys anymore
ever since i realized i was deserving of much more.

al they do is get scared over boss women and run away.
they wouldn't last with a girl like me anyway.

i could've been everything for you and you weren't ready.

i can't allow myself to shed a single tear over you again.

i bossed up heavy.

i just wanted someone who could understand my heart.

thank you for freeing me and allowing someone else treat me like art.

i'm not the type of person to give up on someone so easily.

i will work with you,
learn you,
i'll even try and heal your past wounds
and that's where i've always messed up.

i don't abandon people and just act like there was never a thing
between us.

that's why it hurts when someone gives up so easily on me.

like did i ever even mean anything to you or it was just a fling?

thinking you were different is where i went wrong.

you had me fooled with the fake charm all along.

here i was thinking i had found what was best,

meanwhile you played and overlooked me just like the rest.
i won't waste my time,
i deserve better for myself.

just don't come back when you can't find a vibe like mine in
someone else.

it's okay if you choose someone else.

i'll accept if it's not meant to be.

but just keep in mind that she'll never be me.

she won't ever love you like i can,

hold you down in every way,

lick and caress you like i did.

i could've been everything for you if only you would have let me.

i mean, i remember the way you looked at me the first time you met me.

different, rare, a dream girl you said?

i got it though, you'd rather have me for one night instead.

when you're a good person,
you don't lose people.

people lose you.

it's never a loss.

# Love Notes

i wish the hours could go slow when i'm with you

how is it 12 a.m already.

i don't feel time when i'm with you.

can we just make today last?

make it go in slow motion?

just waste it away with me.

this new chapter is called love.
can you imagine all this time i was praying for someone like you to
the one above?

you make me forget about all the times i was overlooked, forgotten,
and even rejected.

you make me forget about how much my soul had been affected.

now i write love notes and make it clear how much you mean to me.

for this is what i had been waiting for, just like it was meant to be.

i kinda knew i had been missing out on you.
trying to find understanding in someone new.

i was testing out dangerous waters
i even got a little lost in between friends and lovers.

but really all i ever wanted was you.

love doesn't hurt.
love heals.

love doesn't whisper your name one night, then tell you straight lies
the next.

love doesn't sit with you at the bar one day, laughing off a drunken
night.

love holds you down every day
in every way.

it blooms like a flower on the first day of spring
when it's watered with consistency, loyalty, and affection.

remember this.

your arms feel like home.
like a nestled little villa in the city of Rome.

your name tastes like love against my tongue.
what did you do, to get me this sprung?

i like this type of love .. wild, free and young

thank you for making me smile.
i knew someone like you would be worth the while.

i told you about all the scars residing in my heart

.. and still you think i'm made out of art.

come my love
do not be fearful like the rest.

here, just take my hand, let me show you what's best

i love all of you.

i love your flaws that make you, you.

i love your smile, your voice, your scent.

i love the feeling of you in the morning.

your love is contagious.

you make me a better woman.

you motivate me to be the best version of myself i can be.

you keep me going.

you ignite fire in my soul and heart

- *you*

don't go.
stay with me forever.

i know forever sounds like a long time.

but i want you for a long time.

you're everything i ever wanted.

just stay forever.

come my love,
it's never too late for us to start our love all over again.

i know timing was right.
distance wasn't right.

our hearts were so far away.

at one point, i felt like you were in another world.

but it's never too late.

my hearts screams your name.
let's ignite the fire all over again.

the many times i was broken, mean nothing when i'm with you.

i think i had to go through all that so i could heavily appreciate the raw love you had to pour.

this is magnetic. it's unrefined. it's pure.

i'm tired of waiting.
i need to be in your arms now.

you're home,

and i miss home.

come back already.

- *long distance love*

# Self-Love

when you love yourself, you glow from the inside out.

you begin to attract the right people, the right friends, and the right lovers into your life.

your energy of love attracts abundance into your life.

and it all begins with you.

this whole time you've been searching for love and it's right in front of you.

you already have it in you.

it is YOU.

start feeling worthy of yourself and valuable.

be magnetic towards positive and loving energies.
you are the love of your life.

self love is being selective of who you allow into your spirit.

it's knowing when friendships and relationships have an expiration date and need to be removed from your life.

when you're full of self love, you are able to open your heart to the people that deserve your love, and close it to the ones that want to intoxicate your soul.

it's knowing when to shut the door because your heart is not a revolving door for people to walk in and out as they please.

some girls are uncomfortable spending time alone,

and it shows.

jumping at anyone and everyone that gives them an ounce of attention.

mistaking flings for love.

acting like every single crush is the man of your dreams.

you're jumping from guy to guy.
you keep opening your soul and allowing energies to walk in and out.

and it shows.

your lack of self esteem is pouring all over.
that's why you keep getting hurt.

learn to spend some time alone. love yourself first.

that will allow you to properly decipher who is really meant to stay.

you are enough.
express yourself unapologetically and explore the sides of you that
make you truly feel alive.

live each day walking in your purpose, being gentle on yourself,
loving yourself, and being the absolute best version of yourself.

the world needs more girls like you.

soft, yet strong.
quiet, but outspoken in every way.

courageous and unapologetic.

know your worth and begin to attract what you deserve.

knowing your worth is not allowing anything to come and steal your joy.

you deserve nothing but things that make your heart ignite in passion and your soul light up like the sunshine.

knowing your worth includes saying no sometimes.
saying no is a part of self love.

live your best life.

find yourself.

lick all your wounds slowly and step into a path of healing and love
because you deserve nothing less that divinity and unrefined love.

why are you waiting for a person, place, or thing to let you know
what your value is?

search within your soul and find characteristics and qualities that
make you the queen that you are.

you don't wait for a man to see your value.

you don't have to wait for money to define your value.

you have to wake up and see your value for yourself.

it's all inside you queen.

go after that dream. that goal you've always wanted.
you deserve to live the life you've always wanted.

you've been broken for too long.
it's time you start showing up.
not for anyone else, but for yourself.

self love feels different because you never settle for anything that is not for your greatest good.

a man could walk in and out of your life, but guess what, it's his loss, not yours, because you're already filled with love inside.

you don't go looking for love, because it resides inside of you already. say it over and over:

i am love.

i am love.

you came so far all on your own.

you no longer accept things that don't align with your purpose.

you no longer accept things that don't feed your soul

and you no longer accept things that don't fill you with love.

you are strong.

even if you don't feel it at this very moment.

you are strong by default because you are a woman.

you have capabilities and qualities within you that have the potential
to move mountains.

don't ever dim your light to please anyone else.

be that woman that lifts another one up, that speaks her mind
unapologetically, and pours love and wisdom in everything she does.

that is you.

she has a world of love inside of her.

she no longer focuses on things, people, or situations that serve her no purpose.

she is evolving and molding into the woman she was destined to be.

.. and look at you now.
you've been broken.
you healed.
you fell in love all over again

and you learned to love yourself amidst it all.

you did it.

and what a beautiful journey it was.

*... breaking. healing. loving.*

Made in the USA
Middletown, DE
31 July 2019